I Can Read!

READING
3
ALONE

Minnie and Moo
WANTED
DEAD OR ALIVE

Den s cazeT

HarperCollinsPublishers

For Sarah and Anna,
with much affection
—Uncle D.

Library of Congress Cataloging-in-Publication Data
Cazet, Denys.
   Minnie and Moo, wanted dead or alive / by Denys Cazet.— 1st ed.
      p.   cm. — (I can read book)
   Summary: Trying to help Mr. Farmer with his finances, Minnie and Moo go to the bank to ask for money and are mistaken for the Bazooka sisters, dangerous outlaws.
      ISBN-10: 0-06-073010-2 (trade bdg.) — ISBN-13: 978-0-06-073010-9 (trade bdg.)
      ISBN-10: 0-06-073011-0 (lib. bdg.) — ISBN-13: 978-0-06-073011-6 (lib. bdg.)
      ISBN-10: 0-06-073012-9 (pbk.) — ISBN-13: 978-0-06-073012-3 (pbk.)
      [1. Cows—Fiction. 2. Outlaws—Fiction.] I. Title. II. Series.
PZ7.C2985Mmu 2006
[E]—dc22   2005014526

16 17 18   PC/WOR   10 9   ❖

Farmer Trouble

Moo ran past the old oak tree.

She ran past Minnie

and flopped onto a chair.

"Oh my, oh my," she muttered.

"What to do? What to do?"

"What's the matter?" asked Minnie.

"Farmer trouble," said Moo.

"Mr. and Mrs. Farmer
don't have enough money
to pay their bills."
"Relax," said Minnie. "The farmer—"
"Minnie!" said Moo.
"The farmer has no money.
This makes him sad.
He'll get sadder and sadder.
He'll never leave the house.

The crops will go bad.

A dust storm will blow away the barn.

A flood will wash away the farm."

"The town will be washed away.

We'll all be washed away!"

Moo looked at Minnie sadly.

"I never learned to swim," she said.

"Moo!" said Minnie. "Will you stop!

There isn't going to be a flood.

And—"

"Wait!" said Moo.

"I'm having a thought."

Minnie rolled her eyes.

"Trouble," she muttered.

"I see a bank," said Moo.

"I see piles of money. It's extra.

We'll ask them for some."

"Moo!" said Minnie. "We're cows! How are you going to get the bank to give money to a cow?"

"I'll write them a note," said Moo.

The Plan

Minnie followed Moo into the barn.

Moo opened an old trunk.

"Here," she said. "Put these on."

"Moo," said Minnie.

"This is a suit and tie."

"The richer we look," said Moo,

"the more money they'll give us."

Moo handed Minnie a hat
and a pair of sunglasses.
"The bank is on the other side
of town," said Minnie.
"How are we going to get there?"
"We'll borrow the farmer's tractor,"
said Moo, looking around the barn.
"But Moo," said Minnie. "I—"

"Suitcase," said Moo. "We need something to carry the money in." Minnie looked behind the trunk. "What about this?" she asked. "A violin case!" said Moo. "Perfect!"

Wanted

Moo parked the tractor.

They walked into the bank.

"Good morning," said a woman.

She put some money in her purse.

"See?" said Moo.

"When you need money

you go to the bank."

"Look at those posters," said Minnie.

"Those people are WANTED."

"Of course," said Moo.

"They are favorite bank shoppers.

Remember when the market named

Mrs. Wilkerson Shopper of the Year?

They put her picture up."

"But Moo," said Minnie.

"Look at that poster.

The Bazooka sisters

don't look like Shoppers of the Year.

See? It says they're wanted!

They're wanted dead or alive!"

"And . . . look at them!"

added Minnie.

"They look just like us!"

19

Moo sighed.

"Minnie, don't you see?
The bank just wants people
to feel good about themselves.
Even if you're dead," said Moo,
"it's nice to know
you're still wanted."

The Note

Moo walked over to a table.

"Now we write the note," said Moo.

"What will it say?" Minnie asked.

"It will say please," said Moo.

"When you ask a bank for money,

it's important to be polite."

Moo wrote the note.

Dear bank person,

Please fill this case with money.

Thank you.

"There!" said Moo.

"Now we have to wait in line."

When it was their turn,

Moo gave a nice man the note.

He looked at it carefully.

He looked at Minnie and Moo.

He looked at the wanted posters.

"Oh no!" he said.

He gave the note to the manager.

"Good afternoon," the manager said.

"I'm Mrs. Proons. How may I help—"

She stopped.

She looked at Minnie and Moo.
"It's the Bazooka sisters!"
she yelled.

The Robbery

Everyone put their hands up.

"What are they doing?" Minnie asked.

"They're being polite," said Moo.

"It's called customer service."

Minnie held up her arms.

She held up the violin case.

"Ohhh!" everyone gasped.

"Don't make any sudden moves," whispered Mrs. Proons.

"There could be a bazooka in there!"

Minnie opened the violin case.

"Look," someone whispered.

"The case is empty.

Shall I call the police?"

Mrs. Proons looked at Minnie.

Minnie smiled.

She reached under her coat.

"Oh!" moaned Mrs. Proons.

"She's reaching for a bazooka!"

"Quick!" cried Mrs. Proons.

"Fill up the case with money!"

Minnie took out her handkerchief

and blew her nose.

The Great Escape

Minnie put the violin case
on the seat of the tractor.
Moo waved to the nice people
at the bank as they drove away.
"What a beautiful day," said Moo.
"Moo," said Minnie, "I hear a siren."
"There must be a fire," said Moo.

"Moo," said Minnie,

"I see flashing lights!"

"Must be fire trucks," said Moo.

"We had better get out of the way."

"They're getting closer!" said Minnie.

Moo pulled off the road.

"We'll take a shortcut through
Mr. Wilkerson's corn field," she said.
"I hear shooting!" said Minnie.
"Hunting season!" said Moo.

"Oh! Moo, hurry!" said Minnie.
"I don't like being away from
the farm during hunting season."
Moo stepped on the gas!

The Police

Moo parked the tractor.
Minnie put the money
on the farmer's back porch.
They walked back to the barn.
Sirens wailed louder and louder.
The farmer and his wife, Millie,
stepped out onto the porch.

Police cars roared into the yard.

The police chief and Mrs. Proons jumped out of the car.

"The Bazooka sisters just robbed the bank!" shouted the chief.

"What?" said the farmer.

"They used your tractor!"

said Mrs. Proons.

"They took a shortcut

through Wilkerson's corn field."

Millie saw the violin case.

"Why . . . that looks like my old—"

"OH!" yelled Mrs. Proons.

She grabbed the violin case

and hugged it tightly.

"You saved my beautiful money!"

"Come on," said the chief.

"The Bazooka sisters are on foot.

We can still catch them!"

"Wait!" shouted Mrs. Proons.
She opened the violin case
and gave the farmer a dollar.
"Your reward," she said
and jumped back into the car.

The Reward

The farmer looked at the money.

He looked at Millie.

"This morning," he said,

"when we were paying our bills,

we were behind by thirty-five cents.

Now we're ahead by sixty-five cents.

Doesn't that seem a bit odd?"

"Now, John," said Millie.

"Don't look a gift horse

in the mouth."

The farmer looked at the tractor.

He looked at the two cows

sitting under the old oak tree.

"I wasn't thinking about horses,"

said the farmer.

Millie looked at the two cows.

"Oh, John," she said.

"You're not going to blame
the cows again."

"Millie, those two—"

"John," said Millie,

"cows don't drive tractors.

Cows don't rob banks.

Cows are just . . . cows."

"If they're just cows,"

said the farmer,

"why are they wearing sunglasses?"